FOUR STRENGTH LIONS

4SL

The Military Begins

C. J. Gray

MUSCLE
BOOKS

ISBN: 10:0998580708

ISBN-13 978-0-9985807-0-8

Illustrations by C. J. Gray

First Edition

:

DEDICATION

To my family and friends.

For those of you who chose this book, read the whole story and you'll be interested in this. Even if you are a new or old fan of Four Strength Lions, read this and you'll know what it is like being in the military school and the war. Enjoy!

CONTENTS

Characters   i

Prologue   iv

1   It's Training Time   1

2   Practice Training Before War   7

3   Getting Healthier   13

4   More Serious Training to Do   23

5   Meeting Aunt Sarah   37

6   The War Begins   50

7   The Squidmania   58

8   End of the Squid War   73

Activity Puzzles   79

Solutions   91

Acknowledgments   98

CHARACTERS

 Midnight– A lion that takes the lead. Brother of Alan, Peter, and James. Friend of Carla. Soldier in Captain Flint's army.

 Alan– A lion that gets bored sometimes. Jokester and prankster. Fastest runner. Master gamer. Brother of Midnight, Peter, and James. Soldier in Captain Flint's army.

 Peter– A lion that is the strongest of the four lions. Master target shooter. Brother of Alan, Midnight, and James. Soldier in Captain Flint's army.

 James– A lion that is smart and cares about peace and nature. Master cook. Master of foreign languages. Brother of Alan, Peter, and Midnight. Soldier in Captain Flint's army.

 Uncle Alex- The uncle of the four lions. Benevolent and well-known in the city. Best friend of Nicholas. Retired scientist.

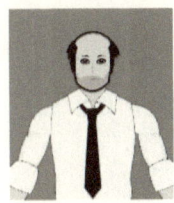 Captain Flint- Captain in the military. Leader of the soldiers. Protector of the city.

 Jake- Friend of Peter and Alan. Soldier in Captain Flint's army.

 Carla- Daughter of Nicholas. Sister of Jackson. Friend of Midnight.

 Aunt Sarah- Aunt of the four lions. Peacemaker.

 Nicholas– Father of Jackson and Carla. Friend of Uncle Alex.

 Jackson– Best friend of Alan. Son of Nicholas. Soldier in Captain Flint's army.

 Nathan– Friend of Peter, Midnight, Alan, and James. Soldier in Captain Flint's army.

 Danny– A wicked lion. Evil genius. Enemy of Uncle Alex and the four lions.

Prologue

Many years ago, in a laboratory *at a top secret base, Dr. Smith mixed together a formula for his scientific experiment. Twelve lions sat in separate cages.*

"We have been testing this formula for the past five years and we're close to a breakthrough discovery. If the formula works, these lions will be able to communicate with humans like no other animal in the history of the world," Dr. Smith explained to a group of military officers.

Dr. Smith injected the twelve lions with the formula and trained them to speak and act like humans. They were not ordinary animals anymore. The military allowed the lions to live and work in a secret community at a top secret base, where they were assigned to work on top secret projects.

One day, Dr. Smith gathered the twelve lions together and said, "We have decided to release you all to go out and live as citizens in a regular community in Atlanta, Georgia. With the training you have been given, you should do well."

Danny and Alex started out as friends, while they learned their jobs as engineers. Alex's job was to build electronics and Danny's job was to build vehicles. They both worked very hard.

One day, while Danny was working, a teenager stole a hammer and keys, using it to smash car windows in every vehicle, until he found a car and drove off spraying paint all over the vehicles.

"Danny, you're fired!" the boss shouted, blaming Danny for letting it happen during his shift.

Danny screamed, "No!" as the cops arrested Danny.

Knowing that Danny was innocent, Alex shouted, "No, don't!"

"Let him go to jail!" the boss shouted at Alex. "Your friend is in trouble! He deserves what he gets! He's a criminal!"

Danny was later arrested and sent to a prison filled with dangerous criminals. During lunchtime, the prisoners taunted Danny every day, and as a result, Danny became angry and resentful. He destroyed the prison and escaped. After his escape, Danny asked Alex to join his nefarious side. Alex refused to join Danny and decided to stay on the good side.

Alex and Sarah married and had a son named Alex Jr and a daughter named Hannah. Sarah's brother, Steven, became a marine soldier. He married Melissa and they had four sons. Melissa often sang lullabies to the four lion cubs.

After singing to them, she would kiss all four lion cubs on their forehead, saying. "Always remember that we love you very much. Your grandparents love you, too, and they want you to grow up to be strong and brave, like your father! He is a brave soldier and you four should be brave too!"

Chapter 1
It's Training Time

After their grandparents died from cancer and their parents moved to Chicago, Illinois, Uncle Alex made plans to send the four lions to military school in order to get stronger. These four lions are named Peter, Midnight, Alan, and James.

One day, while the four lions were watching TV with an antenna, eating cereal, and getting dressed, Midnight asked, "Where are you going, Uncle Alex?"

Uncle Alex answered, "I'm taking you teens to the military school in Atlanta."

Alan and Midnight both wondered what it was like being in military school. They had images of P.E. with some sports, exercising, and lifting weights. Peter imagined himself doing weightlifting and exercising a lot with his friends.

"Just take your time, Peter," Midnight said.

"Oh, I will," said Peter.

After they imagined it, Peter was doing jumping jacks, sit-ups, and push-ups before military school. He counted while exercising so he wouldn't forget how much he did. James helped him by holding his feet while exercising.

"Ah, thank you!" Peter exclaimed, using good manners.

Alan went back to watch T.V. because he liked to watch his cartoons, comedy shows, and entertainment videos. After that, he lay down to relax.

"It's time to go, boys," said Uncle Alex. Uncle Alex opened the door and went outside so he could drive. Then, he told his nephews to get in the SUV.

At the military school in the morning at 8:15 A.M., a

captain was looking at the four lions. He was seriously confused and planned to ask questions about them.

"We already practiced our military lessons with our uncle and aunt, sir," Midnight said, "Are you going to let us get in the military school or not?"

They were all looking at the four lions with a serious look. Uncle Alex hoped that a captain would give his nephews a chance. He will let them go into the military if they can walk or run and do anything that humans would do.

"I saw those lions doing something!" exclaimed Captain Flint. "I can't believe it! You guys may come in and you sir, come here and we'll have a talk about them."

After Captain Flint let the four lions in, he walked straight forward and sat with them. All the soldiers wanted to do was play arm wrestle and card games. But the four lions were different. Whenever they played card games, they refused to gamble over it.

Peter promised himself that, from now on, he would

never gamble or play childish games.

"Wanna play battle?" asked Jake, pointing at Peter. "I promise, I'll let you use rematches for us if you need to."

"Sure, why not!" Peter answered, as he began to play cards with Jake and those soldiers. They were all playing battle for fun.

Reaching for the cards from Jake, Peter began to shuffle. Peter could play any games better than the other soldiers, because the soldiers made mistakes. But, the four lions made few mistakes.

Captain Flint showed up in front of the soldiers, interrupting their game of battle by blowing a loud whistle.

"Time to exercise, boys!" exclaimed Captain Flint. "You guys need to get stronger! Don't act like girls!"

As they all exercised every day, those soldiers began to get healthy and strong. They did jumping jacks, push-ups, mountain climbers, pull-ups, and sit-ups, while drinking protein milk. Captain Flint didn't realize that the four lions could do push-ups and all of those types of exercises.

"Dang! You all did this, really?" Captain Flint questioned while feeling a little astonished about the four lions. "Keep up the excellent work! Now come here for a minute."

Peter and Midnight were interested in fighting and shooting, while Alan and James were interested in peace most of the time.

First, Captain Flint opened the weapon room and next, he showed them guns, shotguns, machine guns, rocket launchers, rifles, and other types of weapons. Finally, he gave those different types of weapons to the four lions. Alan got the rocket launcher. Peter got the machine gun. Midnight got the shotgun. And James got the AK-47.

Captain Flint said, "As soldiers in the military, your

number one duty is to keep our citizens safe. Take these weapons and use them wisely and only as a last resort to protect our people! Is that clear?"

All four lions shouted, "Yes sir!"

Chapter 2
Practice Training Before War

After the four lions received their own guns, they decided to practice shooting. Captain Flint took them inside to teach them how to shoot with real bullets in their weapons. The shooting room was filled with papers that looked like a bull's eye.

Once Captain Flint gave them some ammo for their weapons, the four lions and the other soldiers were ready to shoot. The four lions had never shot a weapon before, since they were new to the military. Before the soldiers began to practice shooting, Uncle Alex showed up in the shooting room, looking at Captain Flint, his nephews, and all the other soldiers.

"Be safe, boys, and don't get yourselves in danger," Uncle Alex commanded his nephews. One-fourth of those soldiers saw Uncle Alex and they didn't know him seriously.

"We promise we won't get ourselves in danger," said Midnight.

"Yeah," Alan said.

Uncle Alex put a peace sign on all of them, especially Captain Flint and his nephews by using his fingers.

The soldiers had never met Uncle Alex. "Is that your dad?" Nathan asked. "Because I didn't know if that was your father or not."

"No, Nate! This is our uncle," said Alan. "His name is Uncle Alex and he is nice and benevolent."

"Yes, he is but how did your uncle learn to act like a human being?" Nathan asked, while feeling amazed.

"I have no idea but he's been doing it for as long as we

can remember," Alan answered Nathan. "He taught us to do everything like this."

"Oh," said Nathan. Nathan understood them very well. He also knew one fact about animals and one fact about them was that they never spoke. That was just how it was. All animals were supposed to speak with their own language.

Peter and Midnight were both prepared for shooting and fighting. They were both courageous and had true courage over their armies.

"Ready and fire!" Captain Flint shouted. Then he said, "We'll have to talk about this, Uncle Alex." Captain Flint went into the office and Uncle Alex followed him.

In the office, Captain Flint seemed to be proud of the four lions. He sat on the chair and looked at Uncle Alex. "I love to say this, Alex. I am very proud of your nephews. How come you and your nephews can do everything and speak while other ordinary animals can't? What the heck!"

Uncle Alex smiled at him and said, "It's a long story of something that happened years ago as part of a top secret experiment. But I'll tell you more about it one day." Uncle Alex went on. "Anyway, I just taught my nephews how to talk and do the same stuff that humans do – like bowling, gaming, watching, washing, exercising, and more."

"And that is why I let them join this military," Captain Flint conceded. "That's really a cool thing to do, Alex. I like that!" Captain Flint thought for a moment about animals who can speak like humans. If he were an animal he would have done it just like Uncle Alex, teaching them to act like humans.

He rose from his chair and left the office. After shooting, the next thing was to teach his soldiers how to fight. "I'll be right back, Alex!" exclaimed Captain Flint.

"Okay, sir," said Uncle Alex.

After leaving the office, Captain Flint walked back to the shooting room to see how well the soldiers were doing with shooting practice.

Captain Flint observed the bull's eye papers in the shooting room. He saw that most of the papers were shot between the white spaces, missing the bull's eye. But a few soldiers had hit the bull's eye, especially Midnight and James. They were both good at shooting things. "You all did an excellent job at shooting!" Captain Flint yelled. "Let's visit to our class!"

"Now this is freaking boring," said Alan. "All of these classes are just a piece of junk!"

Jake agreed with Alan, but Midnight disagreed.

"Alan, this is not boring." Midnight said. "The classroom is where Captain Flint teaches us how to do stuff that gets you healthy before you become a marine soldier,

U.S. Navy soldier, and a normal soldier who was there for an army— things like running a couple of miles, exercising more, ignoring other distracting stuff that drives soldiers nuts, practicing more fighting, and hiding somewhere."

"Well, that seems interesting." Peter said. "I want to be the strongest lion ever of all times!"

"Aaaargh! People these days!" James complained. All that James was worrying about was making the whole world peaceful and safe, taking care of his pets, giving kids peace and quiet, making kids happy, and meditating every single day. He believed in peace rather than war.

Midnight tried to make James understand. "Listen, James, we know that the whole world is chaotic, but you need to get used to this, okay?" He went on, "We'll fix this later."

Chapter 3
Getting Healthier

After they went into the class, Captain Flint and the other captain showed up screaming, "Good morning, class!"

"Good morning, captain," all soldiers said, except Peter. Peter didn't use his good manners because he was only in the mood for being tough and taking care of his health.

Captain Flint continued, "Today, we are going to see the nurse about whether you are getting healthy enough for running a mile and other outdoor activities and training."

The soldiers were listening to Captain Flint until they saw Peter raise his hand up high.

"Hey, captain!" Peter shouted while he raised his hand. "Guess what?"

"Oh well," Midnight said and sighed.

"What were you going to say, Peter?" Captain Flint asked. "I hope you're not making a joke about this!"

"Our uncle told us to run five miles and start fighting a punching bag for practice," said Peter. "Captain, it's kind of a true story about what we did a week ago."

"That's nice. I appreciate that, Peter," Captain Flint said. "Let us all stand up and go see the nurse! Am I clear?"

The soldiers stood up and screamed, "Yes, sir!"

"Now follow me, boys," said Captain Flint. All soldiers followed Captain Flint. They saw three other captains who were on their way to the nurse, too.

When they got in to the nurse's room, the nurse checked to see if all soldiers were healthy enough for outdoor activities.

"I have some questions for you," said Nurse Tanner. "If you're not healthy, then you will have to get out of the military." Then, Nurse Tanner asked, "Can you run a mile?"

"Who? All of us!" James asked. "To four of us, we say yes. We all can run a mile without giving up. Before the military, all we ever did was exercise, drinking a gallon of water every day, hiking, and running."

"I drink eight bottles of water a day," Jake said. "That's what I do, every single day!"

Peter thought that drinking water while doing outdoor activities and exploring nature made people healthy.

"All I did is meditate every day and give people hope and forgiveness," said James.

"That's very sweet, but you have to get healthy," Nathan said.

"Yeah I exercise a little, for training but not that much," James said. "Anyway, what time is it?"

Midnight looked at his wrist watch. "It's 9:35, James,"

he said. "Which means ten minutes left?"

"Yep!" Captain Flint answered. Captain Flint and Nurse Tanner concluded that everyone was prepared for training and running laps before entering the army.

"Peter, hold out your arm," Nurse Tanner said, grabbing the pressure cuff and wrapping it on Peter's arm.

"What does that thing do?" asked Alan. "I hope it's not dangerous."

"It's not dangerous, Alan," said Nurse Tanner. "It checks on our blood pressure to see if we have low or high blood pressure."

Alan asked nicely, "Oh, really!"

"Yes, it does," Nurse Tanner said. Nurse Tanner concluded that Peter had a normal blood pressure and a normal heart rate, which meant that he was very well for outdoor activities.

Next, Nurse Tanner took Peter to a scale to get his weight and height. "6 feet, 6 inches and 167 pounds." Nurse Tanner said.

He did the same for Alan, Midnight, James, and the other soldiers. Alan weighed 149 pounds and his height was 5 feet, 5 inches. Midnight weighed 158 pounds and his height was 5 feet, 7 inches. James weighed 154 pounds and his height was 5 feet, 3 inches.

"Well, I see!" Nurse Tanner said. "It won't be too long before all of you lions are as big as the adults! You guys are free to go! Have a nice day!"

"Peace!" Alan exclaimed, putting two fingers in front of Nurse Tanner while walking away.

Nurse Tanner did the same, putting up two fingers and saying "Peace," as Alan left. Nurse Tanner remained in the nurse's room, waiting for other people who were sick or having some issues and allergies.

After leaving the nurse's room, the soldiers decided to go outside to run laps, climb the mountain, fight punching bags, and other activities.

James had a backpack containing four water bottles. He gave one to each of his brothers and kept one for himself.

"Thanks!" exclaimed Alan. "You are a good brother, you know that!"

"Anytime, Alan," James said.

A person held the door for all soldiers who wanted to go outside. When they got out, all they could see was a track and field and some other training courses far away. The soldiers were ready to run some laps and miles.

One thing about James is that he didn't like to run laps or a mile, because he didn't have enough energy to run. He ran slower, like a grown adult.

"Ready!" Captain Flint shouted. "And run!"

All soldiers were running a lap to get healthy, even the four lions. The soldiers never quit running. Alan was the fastest runner. Nobody could beat him in the race.

"How did you run like that?" asked Jackson. "The way you just ran was totally amazing! I like that!"

"I spent a lot of time using the treadmill for five months when I was like seven or eight," said Alan. "Seriously, like five months!"

"And that's why you run fast like this, right?" Jackson asked to make sure if Alan told the truth or not.

"Yes, I really should've finished already," said Alan. "Please tell me, what's your name?"

"Oh yeah, my name is Jackson!" the soldier exclaimed while grinning. "What's yours?"

"My name is Alan." The two of them shook hands. "Nice to meet you!" Alan said.

"Come on, guys!" Peter warned Alan and Jackson. "Can you both just run? We don't have all stinking day to do this stuff!"

"Maybe you should worry about yourself, Peter." Jake said.

"Oh, shut up Jake!" Peter shouted. "Why don't you worry about yourself!"

"I'm just helping you, Peter," said Jake.

Peter shouted, "Yeah, you're right! We should run!"

Chapter 4
More Serious Training to Do

About thirty minutes later, the soldiers stopped running because Captain Flint told them to stop running and start some training.

Next, Captain Flint said, "For those of you who are new to the military, please pay attention to me and you will learn some skills that I just taught you, but better! I want to teach you some more serious training skills that you will need during the war."

"So which training skills would you like to teach us first?" Peter asked.

Some of them were looking over at Peter.

Peter said while being serious, "Captain, I only asked

that because it was very important for us and Uncle Alex."

"I know, but the first training skill I have to teach all of you is to dodge things," said Captain Flint. "Next, all of you guys have to do some climbing."

"Well, the four of us have never climbed before." Midnight said.

Jake said, "Me neither. I never climbed before in my whole entire life."

"Me neither," Jackson said.

Everyone had joined in the conversation telling whether they had climbed before or not.

Captain Flint overheard and yelled, "Silence!"

"All right! Let's do some training." Captain Flint said. Then Captain Flint and the soldiers walked toward the training courses.

"This is going to be so much fun!" Peter shouted excitedly.

"Get serious, Peter!" Midnight shouted.

"Sorry, I can't help myself. I just like to do all the training," said Peter.

"It's okay! I forgive you, Peter," Midnight said. "But you need to get serious, you know."

"These are the training courses that you all are about to do." Captain Flint said. "If you're able to just make it all the way, you're in luck. If not, then try again and practice some more. Am I clear?"

All soldiers shouted, "Yes, sir!" to Captain Flint.

The first training course that the soldiers did was to dodge things. "Now if you see something that's trying to hit you, just dodge it," Captain Flint said. "Let's get started!"

The objects that came at them consisted of wood, metal, fake guns, and grenades filled with smoke. Every time they saw an object, they dodged it just to avoid getting hurt.

The soldiers ran fast and did what Captain Flint told them to do. The four lions were able to do everything that most of the soldiers did. All of the soldiers did a great job at dodging things.

The next training course for them to do was running a mile. To them, it seemed to take them thirty minutes to run a mile.

Captain Flint suddenly realized that the four lions were running on two legs. Captain Flint exclaimed excitedly, "This is exactly why I believe in them because they're the four strength lions!"

With one tear in his eye, Captain Flint just smiled.

"Why are you crying, Captain?" asked Nathan.

"Because I'm very happy for what those lions did," Captain Flint cried with full joy. "This is exactly why I'm happy for them."

Nathan said, "Oh, I get it." He continued running a whole mile with the lions and soldiers. After they finished running the mile, they decided to take a break because they had been running for thirty minutes.

"You know what?" asked James. "We'll never give up on those training courses ever. So, we are staying in the military."

While flying in an airplane overhead, Danny saw the four lions and the other soldiers at the military school.

"Training, huh!" Danny exclaimed wickedly. "As soon as I see them, I will toast and demolish them all like a boss!" Danny was busy thinking of plans that might defeat the four lions. "It is on!" Danny shouted with an evil smile. "This might be a sweet revenge on Uncle Alex! I've been meaning to get even with him for a long time!"

Danny looked over at his teammates and he asked, "Are you guys with me or not?"

His teammates understood and followed his orders. They said, "Yes, Danny!"

"Well good," said Danny. "Maybe one day or next week, we'll destroy them together!"

During the military school, the soldiers and the four lions were taking a break.

"So you're ready for the next training course, yet?" asked Captain Flint.

"Not yet, captain," Alan said. "We still need more time."

"All right," said Captain Flint. "I'm just making sure you guys or girls are ready or not."

It was then that Alan saw an airplane. It was so unexpected that he screamed and shouted, "I saw an airplane, I swear!"

"I don't know what's going on but this must be something!" Alan continued screaming. "Like seriously, you have to believe me."

"Dude, relax." Jackson said. "It's just an airplane, there's no need for you to panic."

"Oh, I'm sorry for freaking out, guys." Alan said.

As the airplane flew overhead, Danny set up a giant bomb on a bridge by using a lighter. He lit the string and ten seconds later, there was a loud explosion.

"Oh shoot! What the flip!" shouted Alan.

"Oh heck no," said James. "This is really screwed up. Alan's right about this!"

Peter said, "Who cares! I'm ready for the next mission or training course to complete." Peter hadn't even noticed that the bridge had exploded. All that he cared about was doing more training courses.

"Are you guys sure you're ready for the next mission or a training course?" asked Captain Flint.

"Yes! I'm always ready for it!" Peter shouted excitedly.

"Me too!" said Alan and Jake. "We're all ready for it!"

"That's all I wanted to hear!" Captain Flint shouted. "Now, all of you have to do it!"

The last training course left for them to do was climbing. All soldiers had to practice climbing, since they had never been climbing before, except for Midnight and Alan. They knew how to climb ladders and ropes from watching others do it. Alan learned it by playing so many video games and Midnight learned it by watching some T.V. shows.

"This is how you climb, guys." Midnight said. "Just look at us doing it." Midnight and Alan were showing them how to climb a rope and a ladder.

"Dang! Those lions can even do that, too?" Captain Flint was shocked. "Wow!"

"So that's how you do it," Peter said. "Well thanks for teaching us that! I know how to climb now."

"Then why didn't you do it?" Jake asked.

"It's easy, no big deal," Peter said. He knew how to climb, but he remembered what Uncle Alex had said a few years ago. His uncle told the four lions that if they went into nature, they need to watch out for snakes, boars, bears, alligators, monkeys, armadillo, cliffs, and some terrains like rocky mountains. But Peter had observed that whenever Captain Flint blew a whistle, the soldiers just went ahead carelessly every time.

And now the soldiers were doing it continually. Captain Flint blew his whistle and the soldiers started climbing the rope up where the bridge was.

Alan was the fastest climber as well. "Wait for us, Alan!" Jake shouted.

"Okay, I am," said Alan.

They were almost done climbing up the rope and Alan was still waiting for them.

"I'm done!" screamed Peter. All of the soldiers were done climbing the rope.

"Well, you all completed your training," said Captain Flint. "You all can leave now."

"Thank goodness!" exclaimed James.

"I know right!" said Alan. "This takes me like hours to complete this."

Some of the soldiers were leaving and going out to eat lunch. Uncle Alex was also leaving the military school and his nephews followed him.

"Wait for me guys!" Jake said, following Uncle Alex and the four lions.

Uncle Alex stopped walking and started looking at Jake.

"Can I go with these four lions?" asked Jake.

"Sure." Uncle Alex said. "You may follow my nephews but as a friend to them. Do not get us in trouble, okay."

"I got it!" Jake exclaimed as they got into Uncle Alex's SUV and left the military school. "You're the best animal I've ever met!"

.

Chapter 5
Meeting Aunt Sarah

"So where are we going?" Jake asked, as Uncle Alex drove down Interstate 75.

"We're going to the restaurant to meet my wife, Sarah," Uncle Alex answered. "It's not that far away."

"Oh yeah, let's go there!" exclaimed Jake.

"Where are our portables?" Alan asked James. "Let's play some video games."

James grabbed their portables and game cartridges and said, "I got it, so take these games."

Alan grabbed the portables and gaming cartridges out of James's backpack and gave them to Midnight, Peter, and Jake.

"Thanks, Alan!" Jake exclaimed.

"Anytime!" Alan shouted. They all played video games.

"I think we're almost there, boys," Uncle Alex said.

"Oh, I see," said Jake. "You have some great driving skills!" He didn't realize that Uncle Alex drove so well.

"I've been driving since I was sixteen," said Uncle Alex. "The first time I drove, I was scared a little bit but I never gave up. All I did was focus on some streets every time I drove and then after that, the driver's education teacher realized that I had passed the driving test. I was really proud of myself for passing the driving test. I ended up getting a driver's license."

"Okay, I understand about this, but do I have to do the same thing that you did when you first drove?" asked Jake.

"Yes, if you want to," Uncle Alex said. "You can get out of the SUV, now. We're here!"

"Okay, Uncle Alex!" Midnight shouted.

The four lions hopped out of Uncle Alex's SUV and grabbed their portables.

"Be careful!" exclaimed Uncle Alex. "You four can play video games later, so stop playing games and watch the road and the sidewalk."

"I'm coming, Uncle Alex!" Alan shouted, running to avoid getting hit by a car.

Midnight, Peter, James, and Jake ran too, just as Alan had done.

"Good grief!" exclaimed Uncle Alex. "I'm glad you guys are safe."

"I know," James said.

"Guys, watch me break down the door!" shouted Alan. "One, two, three, Go!"

"No, don't do it!" James and Midnight said.

Alan screamed and ran toward the door as fast as he could run. He was about to smash through the door but the glass cracked a little causing some items to move.

"Ouch!" Alan complained, rubbing his forehead.

"I told you not to do it!" Midnight yelled at Alan. "Why the heck do you do this crap? That's fricking ridiculous!"

"My brothers used to do that when we were the same age as you," said Uncle Alex. "I remember this! It was a long time ago. My friends were there too at the high school. Ah, good times!" Uncle Alex opened the door and saw other people at the restaurant.

The restaurant was all tidy and filled with adults, children, and senior citizens, which meant it was a nice restaurant. They were looking for Aunt Sarah because they wanted to see her. Alan found her table.

"Ah, I see her!" Alan exclaimed a little louder. "She's right here!" They followed Alan.

"Oh, hi guys!" shouted Aunt Sarah, excited to see them.

"Hi, Aunt Sarah!" exclaimed the four lions and their friends.

"So how's the military?" Aunt Sarah asked.

"We'll say the military was great," said Midnight. "All of the exercises and training, it totally helps us to become brave soldiers."

Peter said with excitement, "Yes, we are learning how to fight and shoot a bull's eye with weapons! It's really epic!"

"And we're learning how to dodge, climb, and jump," James added.

"Well, I love to hear that!" Aunt Sarah said. "It's really good to see you!" Aunt Sarah began to shake hands with Midnight, Peter, Alan, James, Jake, and Uncle Alex.

"I usually run fast as a race car so yeah, I'm really healthy enough to run," said Alan.

The waitress was coming towards them and asked, "Can I take your orders?"

Alan ordered a steak, mashed potatoes, corn, and rice.

Peter ordered the fish, an order of shrimp, and a cup of water with it. Midnight ordered some hamburger meat covered with bell peppers, green beans, asparagus, and a Dr. Pepper. James ordered spaghetti and meatballs, broccoli, green beans, a slice of cornbread, and a Pepsi. Jake ordered a hamburger, jambalaya, asparagus, and a 7UP. Uncle Alex ordered four hot dogs, a chicken salad with ranch, and a cup of water. "Done!" Alan, Jake, and James said it all together, putting down the menus.

After the waitress left, they continued their conversation with each other. Uncle Alex said, "When you go to war, just stay brave and help protect each other. Help your teammates to survive and avoid being captured."

"I will be brave and use my weapons," Peter said. "I'm not letting people down, all right."

They went back to playing video games on their portables.

In the kitchen, the waitress told the chef their orders. Twenty to thirty minutes later, the waitress grabbed their plates and gave them to Aunt Sarah, Uncle Alex, his nephews, and Jake first and then to the other people.

"We're so lucky!" Alan exclaimed. After that, they all opened their plates to check and see if they received the right orders. The food looked good. Peter tried it and the fish tasted really good. "This fish tastes way better than Midnight's way of cooking fish."

"You liked it?" asked James.

"Yeah, I did!" Peter shouted excitedly as he was banging the table. "I really like the fish and the shrimp!"

"Jake, I'm on level twenty now," said Alan. "I'll complete this game when I get back outside."

"So you still know how to play this game?" Jake asked. "If you do, then you must practice a lot!"

"Yes," Alan answered. "This game is a little hard. We'll see if I can make it to Level twenty-one or not."

"Well yeah you might try," said Jake.

While Uncle Alex and the four lions were at the restaurant, Danny was outside at the pawn shop to buy weapons and explosives like a couple of sticks of dynamite, bombs, and grenades. He spent hundreds of dollars on the weapons.

"Really! Why did you buy that?" asked Nicholas. "You can't really be planning to do that!"

"Don't worry about it, smarty-pants!" Danny shouted, fussing at Nicholas. "It's not your business! It's my own business and you don't need to know about it!" Danny grabbed the explosives and left.

Nicholas stopped him and screamed, "You are not going to blow up the whole city! I swear, Danny!"'

Danny punched Nicholas in the face really hard and yelled, "My explosives, my fricking property! I'm getting the heck out of this pawn shop, so shut your stinking mouth!" After he punched Nicholas in the face and yelled straight at him, Danny left the pawn shop and ran towards his van, calling his teammates to get in the van.

Nicholas called 911 to report Danny.

"Now it's time to do some serious business and have some more action," said Danny. "No more fun and games!"

"That's what we're talking about, Danny!" Danny's teammates shouted with excitement. "You are an awesome leader!"

"Let's do this!" Danny shouted with excitement. Danny started his own van. He knew how to drive, but chose to drive very fast and crash cars for no reason.

Danny backed up his van at a fast speed, wrecking several vehicles in the parking lot. Then he drove straight into Nicholas's car, crashing the door so hard that it set off the car alarm with a loud noise.

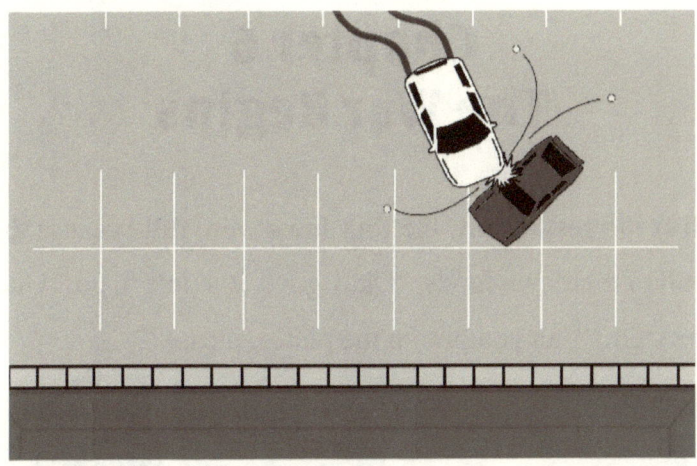

Nicholas left the pawn shop carrying a dartboard that he had purchased. Once outside, he was shocked when he saw the damage to his car. Nicholas slammed down his dartboard in anger. "Darn it!"

Chapter 6
The War Begins

Still at the restaurant, the four lions were full because they ate all of their own foods. "Okay guys, it's time to go," Uncle Alex said. "Can you put up the plates, please?"

"Sure!" James said. "I'll put it up for you."

"No, I got this!" the dishwasher said. "You may leave now, amigo."

When they left the restaurant, all they could see was some buildings that had been exploded by Danny. "This doesn't make any sense!" Jake shouted. "I didn't know this was happening! Darn!"

Aunt Sarah and the customers began running to get away from danger.

Uncle Alex, his nephews, and Jake began to run to get inside of Uncle Alex's SUV. "Get in! Get in!" yelled Peter. "It's time to stop Danny!"

After they got in Uncle Alex's SUV, Alan saw a green truck and a bunch of police cars chasing Danny. He could hear the police sirens, fire truck sirens, and ambulance sirens all together.

Uncle Alex started his SUV, backed up, and began driving away.

At that moment, Nicholas showed up driving Jackson's truck. He found Uncle Alex outside of the restaurant.

They were putting their windows down for an important thing to say.

Nicholas said, "Uncle Alex, please stop Danny from destroying buildings and bridges."

Uncle Alex said, "We'll stop him." They put their windows back up and began to drive away.

At an undisclosed location between the top secret military base and the military school, the soldiers were watching the news on the TV. The news reporter said,

"Breaking News, seven buildings exploded and a bridge was broken down and you know who destroyed it. That lion's name is Danny. He did it for no reason. Kids and adults were screaming because of this."

Captain Flint asked, "Who the heck is Danny? Can somebody please tell me what the heck is going on with this lion? He's destroying the whole city!"

Uncle Alex explained, "Remember that top secret experiment I told you about? Danny was part of that experiment too. He can talk and act like humans. Except, he's evil and destructive. We have to stop him."

Captain Michael, the captain at the top secret base, shut the TV off and forced all soldiers to go out and attack Danny and his teammates. They ran and got into their tanks, vans, military trucks, heavy duty trucks, regular trucks, and four wheel drive jeeps.

Most of the soldiers were driving their vehicles that came from the military. They drove very fast and some of them were using weapons filled with big bullets.

All the soldiers could hear the news reporter on the radio. The news reporter said, "Danny exploded seven buildings and a bridge. It'll be helpful if a group from the military can stop them before Danny takes control and destroys the USA! This is a serious situation but don't forget to protect yourselves from destruction!"

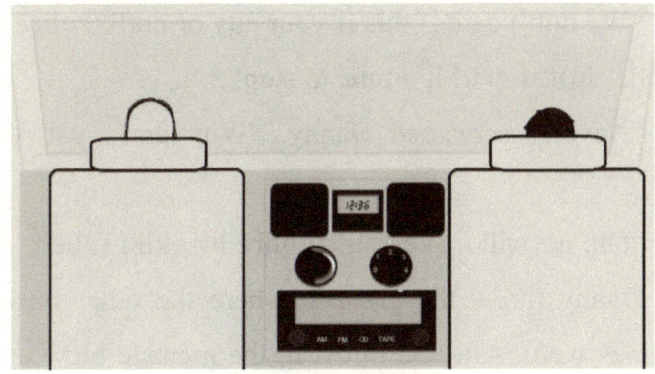

Back from Atlanta, Georgia at 1:15 P.M., the police cars were around Danny's van, which means the police officers found Danny. Danny ran away and tried to use a rocket launcher to explode more buildings. The cops interrupted him, yelling "Freeze!"

Danny surrendered after they yelled at him. "What in the world is wrong with you!" Danny screamed, arguing with the cops and raging. "I don't know why you're doing this to me, but this is my city!"

"We don't care if this is your city or not!" Police Ivor argued. "Just stop it! It's time to stop!"

"Never!" screamed Danny. "Why don't you make me!"

"Oh, we will make you!" Police Franklin yelled.

Danny threw the grenade where the other business buildings were. After he threw it, the grenade blew up the buildings, the roads, the vehicles, taxis, police cars, ambulances, and fire trucks.

"You're asking for trouble, buddy!" Police Ivor yelled at Danny, but Danny ignored the cops.

Danny went into his van, driving it, and transforming the van into an airplane. "Catch that, suckers!" Danny yelled and laughed at the cops.

"This isn't over!" shouted Uncle Alex. "You heard me! We'll destroy you!"

Chapter 7
The Squidmania

Danny pressed the button labeled, "Create Squids." After he pressed it, the alien squids were created and arrived at 1:42 P.M. It was raining squids everywhere, spilling the squid inks down.

"Ah man, what a huge mess!" said Uncle Alex, face palming himself. "Well, let's shoot these squids up!" Within two minutes, about half of the squids jumped high and tried to bite people's head off.

"What you're waiting for?" Captain Flint asked. "We must stop these stupid squids from attacking our people! Kill the baby squids first and then the giant, king squid! Make them die or something!"

All of the soldiers began shooting up squids and saving

the people. Alan saw a man in exercise clothes walking, while listening to music on his cell phone. The man panicked when he saw the squids falling from the sky.

Alan began to run toward the man. "Alan, where the heck are you going!" Captain Flint shouted. "Yeah, go save that man!"

Alan ran at lightning speed. Using a hunting knife, he cut a squid that was trying to bite the man.

"Oh, thank you. You're a true hero!" the man said. "What the heck was that? It stings like a scorpion!"

"No problem, man!" said Alan. "It was a squid!"

"Oh, that's what it is," the man said. Alan heard tree limbs swinging from someone touching it.

Suddenly, Danny's teammate, Chuck, jumped from behind a nearby bush.

"You're dead meat, Alan!" Chuck shouted with anger.

"Not this time, punk!" Alan shouted, as he surprised

Chuck with a jump kick to the chin.

In a park nearby, James saw some of the squids jump up and onto a little girl's head. Kids and teens began screaming and leaving the park in fear, because of this. James ran over to save the little girl. He cut the squid off of her by using a hunting knife.

"Thank you, lion!" the little girl shouted excitedly. "By the way, my neck feels itchy right now."

"You are very welcome, but run free!" James said, full of calm and patience.

As the little girl left the park, a motorcycle showed up. It was Tony, one of Danny's teammates. He came there to challenge James.

"James, come and face me like a man!" screamed Tony. "It's time to fight!"

James wasn't scared, but he took Tony seriously. When Tony swung his fist at him, James blocked his swing.

"What!" Tony shouted. "What kind of fighting style is that?"

"You'll find out!" said James, as he landed a tornado kick to Tony's chest. The powerful force of his kick sent Tony crashing to the ground.

As the soldiers travelled throughout the city shooting up the squids, they encountered a high school that was infested with squids. "Peter, you have to save the students at the school!" yelled Jake.

"All right, fine!" Peter screamed at Jake. "I'll take good care of the students at the school. So, just keep killing squids or else everyone is dead."

"Be very careful!" Jake said.

Peter ran straight down to the high school.

A bus driver had arrived to school early, after seeing a news broadcast about Danny. The reporter said, "Danny is destroying everything. The city is doomed."

"All right, guys!" the teacher said excitedly to the students. "You may dismiss now! Have a great weekend!"

The students felt very glad to be out of school. They repeated "No school!" eight times, burst the door open, and ran to the bus in excitement.

At that time, a squid attacked a teenaged boy who was getting onto a bus at the high school. Peter saw this and raced toward the child, using his hunting knife to cut the squid off.

"Thank you so much!" the teenaged boy said.

As a group of squids swarmed around the school bus, Peter charged toward them. "You're dead meat!" Peter shouted. He pulled out a gun and began shooting up all of the squids. "Darn it! We ran out of bullets!" he screamed. "We're totally doomed!"

"Relax!" Nicholas said. "I'll get my bullets and some ammo for you!" When he returned, Nicholas dropped the box of bullets to the ground.

Peter grabbed the bullets. "Okay, thanks for the bullets and ammo!" he shouted. "And where did you get these from? This kind of ammo seems cheap!"

"I bought it at the pawn shop, no offense," said Nicholas. "This stuff cost me like five dollars."

"Okay, we accept those bullets!" Alan said.

The four lions started shooting up squids to stop them from attacking people all over the city. Midnight ran and began to call Nicholas and his brothers for help. "You guys shoot the squids while I find and save the girl I just fell in love with!"

"Go ahead and save her, brave lion!" Alan screamed excitedly. "We believe you can do it!"

After that, Midnight saw the girl screaming as she ran away from squids.

Midnight ran faster and yelled, "I'm coming to save you, sweetheart!"

The squid followed the girl and tried to bite her as she continued screaming.

"Get off of her, you jerk!" Midnight screamed and stabbed a squid with a knife.

"Ah, thanks!" the girl said. She turned around and saw Midnight, but she was scared of him. She was scared because she thought Midnight would attack or eat her.

"I'll save you, I promise!" Midnight said. "Just wait for a minute!" Midnight kept running. He never gave up.

One of Danny's teammates, Spike, threw a soldier off of a tank. Afterwards, he stole the tank and drove away, speeding through a crowded street firing the missiles. Spike destroyed eleven vehicles, the high school, a garden shop, and a fast-food restaurant. As Spike approached the library, he blasted off with a machine gun, firing shots everywhere. The computers were broken, the lights were out, and the books were ruined. People ran and cried in fear for their lives. As Nathan ran towards the library, Spike blasted off again.

"Move it, guys!" Captain Flint yelled. "We found some better hiding places!"

"Yes, Captain!" all the soldiers said. All the soldiers were running and finding their own hiding places for safety. There were about seventeen places to hide.

Spike drove into the bank and destroyed the entire bank. Jumping from the tank in anger, Spike got mad and ran toward Nathan. He swung at Nathan, but Nathan blocked it and started punching him in the stomach.

"Is everyone hiding?" asked Captain Flint. "Where the heck is Midnight?"

"Oh yeah, he's going to save his girl." Alan answered.

"You mean my sister, right?" asked Jackson.

"Yes!" Captain Flint answered. "We hope that Midnight has luck!"

"I know, right!" said Jackson, smiling at Captain Flint. "Midnight has a crush on Carla and I was impressed." While they were talking about it, they continued shooting squids to death.

Midnight and Carla were inside of the building. A business person closed the door so squids wouldn't get into their way. "Wait! Come back!" shouted Midnight. "Everything is going to be just fine! Just chill the heck out!"

As Carla ran through the building, she grabbed a walking cane from an old lady on the stairs. Afterwards, the old lady fell down through the stairs, crying and screaming for help. "Somebody, please help me!" the old lady cried.

"I'm sorry!" Carla whispered and apologized to the old lady, while being shocked. But, she kept running, without helping the old lady.

Midnight and the other business man picked the old lady up and helped her to walk.

"Thank you!" said the old lady. "You realize that this lady is really crazy! I can't stand her!"

"Yeah, me too!" said the business man. "You're darn right. She's crazy."

Carla stopped to rest on the top floor, looking at the glass windows.

"What are you doing here?" the boss asked. "I need you to go somewhere else. This place is for business people only, not some nuts and silly youngsters like you!"

Carla raised the stick in front of them and yelled at the

boss. "You don't understand! I just want to be safe!"

"Okay, ma'am! We get it!" shouted the boss. "Just drop the stick, okay! Don't you even dare hit us with a stick!"

As Carla dropped the stick, the business men were staring and whispering about her.

Danny flew his airplane closer to the building and hovered.

The boss yelled, "Everybody get yourselves down and get to the fricking corner and walls, right now!"

Carla and the business men and women were trying to get closer to the corners and the walls, before Danny got a chance to shoot the glass windows and set a bomb to the top floor.

After that, Danny was able to shoot the glass with a machine gun. The glass shattered.

Suddenly, Midnight burst through the elevator door, using his powerful kick and ran out of the elevator.

Danny threw a grenade at the top floor.

"All of you got twelve seconds, climb up the ladder!" Midnight shouted.

"Stop following us, you idiot lions!" Carla yelled at Midnight and Danny.

Danny grabbed the megaphone and shouted, "Come to papa, Midnight!"

"Not a chance!" Midnight yelled at Danny and climbed the ladder really quick. Finally, he made it to the top of the building.

Chapter 8
End of the Squid War

"Are you sure you can handle this?" asked the boss.

"Yes, I can handle this sir!" answered Midnight. The top floor had already exploded.

"Well good!" the boss said. "Just do it, already!"

"I am doing it!" Midnight screamed. Suddenly, Midnight heard his walkie-talkie turn on automatically.

"Are you safe, Midnight?" Captain Flint asked on the

walkie-talkie.

"Yes, I'm safe!" Midnight shouted back to Captain Flint, using his walkie-talkie.

"Good!" said Captain Flint, using his walkie-talkie. "We're trying to kill the giant squid so just stay safe, okay! I don't want you to die against Danny!"

"Who the heck was that?" Carla asked Midnight. "Wasn't that one of your teammates?"

"That's my Captain!" Midnight answered to Carla and smiled at her.

Carla smiled back at Midnight and said, "Okay!"

"Just do what I said or I'll steal your girl!" Danny yelled at Midnight.

"Fine!" Midnight screamed. "I'll do it, all right!"

"No, don't you dare!" shouted the boss. "He's going to get you hurt!"

Then, Midnight shot Danny's plane, causing it to explode.

"Oh my goodness!" exclaimed Jackson and Captain Flint as they saw Danny's plane explode.

Danny fell down to the ground, screaming for help.

"Yep, he deserves to fall down after his plane got exploded," Alan said. "We're glad to see that happen!" The top part of the building shook.

"Oh no! This floor is about to collapse!" screamed Midnight. "Just hold tight, everyone!"

"That's right! You heard the lion, people!" the boss screamed. "All you have to do is hold tight!"

Midnight saw a zip line and a bunch of zip line handle bars.

"All right, everybody!" Midnight shouted. "Let's slide down!"

They all grabbed and held their zip line handle bars and began to slide themselves down. They went back to where Captain Flint and the other soldiers were.

"I'm glad you guys are safe," said Captain Flint.

"So what's your name?" Midnight asked.

"My name is Carla." she answered. "What's yours?"

"My name is Midnight," he answered. "Great to see you, Carla!"

"Nice to see you too!" Carla shouted excitedly. "I can't believe you saved my life, Midnight!" Midnight and Carla hugged each other.

"You did a fantastic job there, Midnight!" Captain Flint said and cried with tears of joy. "And you all did great! Keep it up!"

"Thanks, Captain!" Alan, Peter, James, and Jake said.

Uncle Alex showed up and saw his nephews, his nephew's friends, and the soldiers walking back to the military school.

Hundreds of people were hurt during the squid war. The firefighters were there to extinguish the fire using a hose of water. The doctors were there to pick up people and take them to the hospital. Some police officers were arresting Danny and his teammates.

The war was over, but the city would never be the same again. But the four lions will be there with the rest of the army, keeping the city at peace and safe from destruction.

4SL
ACTIVITY PUZZLES

Puzzle 1

Word Search

P	X	E	L	A	E	L	C	N	U
R	E	T	E	P	H	H	Z	T	B
T	H	H	I	N	A	T	Y	J	Q
Y	E	U	W	A	R	H	Z	A	M
N	S	K	G	L	A	G	E	M	J
N	L	J	A	A	S	I	N	E	U
A	P	S	O	J	T	N	P	S	Z
D	Q	K	E	L	N	D	G	Z	S
Y	C	R	N	N	U	I	B	J	C
I	H	T	I	S	A	M	B	T	X

Danny	Jake	Aunt Sarah
Uncle Alex	Alan	James
Peter	Midnight	

Puzzle 2

Word Search

H	R	Q	B	Y	C	T	V	Y	M
T	V	P	X	R	A	N	L	J	V
O	Z	I	K	A	R	A	E	P	S
P	S	K	C	T	L	R	Y	A	A
S	Y	H	I	I	A	U	E	W	L
E	D	A	J	L	W	A	S	N	O
C	R	I	P	I	G	T	L	S	H
R	T	F	U	M	K	S	L	H	C
E	A	Z	S	Q	N	E	U	O	I
T	U	X	I	U	S	R	B	P	N

Carla	Nicholas	Squids
Bull's Eye	Restaurant	Pawn Shop
Military	Top Secret	

Puzzle 3

Word Search

E	S	I	C	R	E	X	E	A	P
C	L	I	M	B	I	N	G	E	T
G	N	I	N	I	A	R	T	N	E
I	B	H	E	S	R	U	N	A	A
G	L	F	E	A	I	E	L	L	M
Z	W	H	Z	A	F	T	M	P	M
W	N	K	P	G	L	K	I	R	A
H	R	V	H	V	U	T	K	I	T
G	N	I	G	D	O	D	H	A	E
E	N	I	L	P	I	Z	N	Y	S

Airplane　　　Training　　　Exercise

Healthy　　　Nurse　　　Climbing

Dodging　　　Teammates　　　Zip Line

Puzzle 4

Crossword

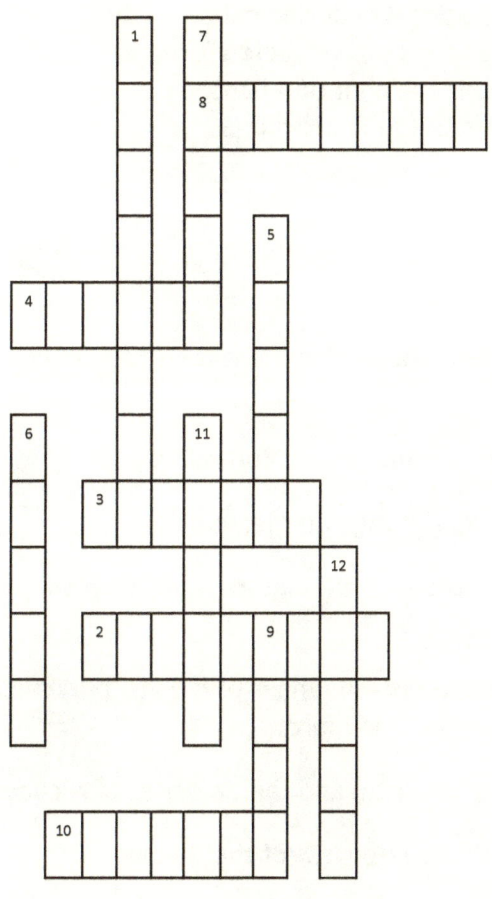

Across

2. A lion who is the uncle of 4 lions.
3. Name of the city where 4 lions and the soldiers were exercising and having war during military school.
4. Danny pressed the button labeled "Create _____"
8. A lioness who is the aunt of 4 lions.
10. A man who is the son of Nicholas.

Down

1. A lion who takes the lead and obeys Captain Flint's orders.

5. A captain who trained 4 lions for military.

6. A lion who is full of rage and jealousy.

7. A lion who likes peace and nature more than chaos and destruction.

9. A lion who is the fastest runner of 4 lions, plays video games, board games, and more.

11. A girl who is beautiful and the daughter of Nicholas.

12. A lion who is the strongest of the 4 lions.

Puzzle 5

Word Search

E	S	L	H	Z	V	N	H	H	N
S	Q	P	P	S	A	S	S	A	E
E	Q	H	V	M	H	I	I	U	S
U	I	R	R	I	N	L	L	F	E
G	F	E	N	A	A	Z	G	H	N
U	G	D	P	T	S	X	N	K	A
T	I	S	I	N	P	R	E	B	P
R	L	N	A	I	S	S	U	R	A
O	E	S	E	N	I	H	C	A	J
P	H	C	N	E	R	F	B	R	O

Italian	Hindi	Russian
Portuguese	German	Japanese
Chinese	French	Spanish
English		

Puzzle 6

Word Search

S	E	O	T	A	T	O	P	G	C
P	Q	U	H	S	I	F	A	R	O
E	C	I	R	L	G	J	Y	E	R
O	F	U	K	F	U	P	A	E	N
J	N	N	N	A	G	M	L	N	B
D	R	F	H	L	S	I	A	B	R
A	O	Q	N	T	V	R	B	E	E
L	C	B	E	O	N	H	M	A	A
A	A	A	D	D	C	S	A	N	D
S	K	J	F	Z	K	E	J	S	N

Steak	Potatoes	Corn
Rice	Fish	Shrimp
Green Beans	Jambalaya	Cornbread
Salad		

Puzzle 7

Word Search

```
S   K   E   P   Z   X   M   G   E   C
Y   H   G   N   I   N   N   U   R   L
S   O   O   S   I   T   U   P   S   I
N   P   D   O   D   G   I   N   G   M
N   Z   U   J   T   X   V   P   N   B
F   I   G   H   T   I   N   G   I   I
J   C   E   E   S   G   N   X   K   N
J   H   I   Z   Z   U   M   G   I   G
R   B   Z   W   D   B   P   D   H   Z
I   U   W   S   Q   U   A   T   S   Y
```

Sit Ups   Push Ups   Squats

Dodging   Climbing   Running

Hiking   Fighting   Shooting

Puzzle 8

Word Search

P	I	H	S	E	L	T	T	A	B
B	E	N	I	R	A	M	B	U	S
O	K	C	U	R	T	H	N	D	R
M	Z	U	V	P	U	D	X	P	D
B	V	Y	J	M	D	K	K	S	X
E	C	E	V	L	N	V	N	W	O
R	E	E	J	F	U	S	P	A	J
P	E	Z	X	S	B	Q	S	I	T
T	E	J	R	E	T	H	G	I	F
R	E	T	P	O	C	I	L	E	H

Humvee   Jeep   Battleship

Helicopter   Tank   Truck

Bomber   Fighter Jet   Submarine

Puzzle 9

Word Scramble

1. WRA _____
2. IMTRYLIA _____
3. GTNNIARI _____
4. MINGCBIL _____
5. IDODGNG _____
6. GFITHGIN _____
7. NUNIRGN _____
8. NHTOOGSI _____
9. NEUCL XAEL _____
10. NMTIDHIG _____
11. RPETE _____
12. LAAN _____
13. SJMAE _____
14. ATCPNIA IFTLN_____
15. NOAHICSL _____
16. COJKANS _____
17. JEKA _____
18. HNNAAT _____

Puzzle 10

Word Scramble

1. UTNA RHSAA _____

2. ANDNY _____

3. TYNO _____

4. UKCCH _____

5. 7KA4- _____

6. IHEAMCN GNU _____

7. NSHUGOT _____

8. RTECOK HRNCULAE _____

9. SUQISD _____

10. NALATTA _____

11. IAHOCCG _____

12. TEESRINTTA _____

13. ATKN _____

14. UKCTR _____

15. LSPETBHIAT _____

16. EBBRMO _____

17. HVEOME _____

18. PEEJ _____

SOLUTIONS

Puzzle 1

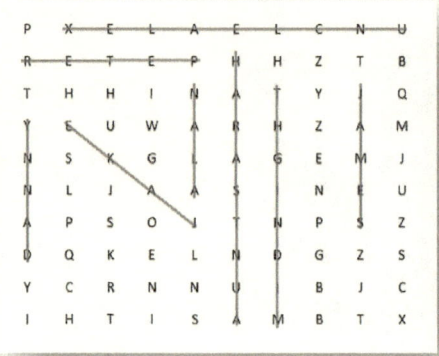

Puzzle 2

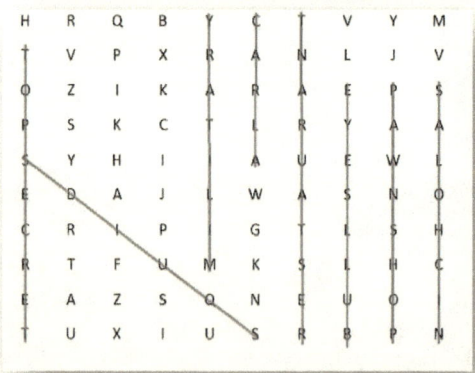

Puzzle 3

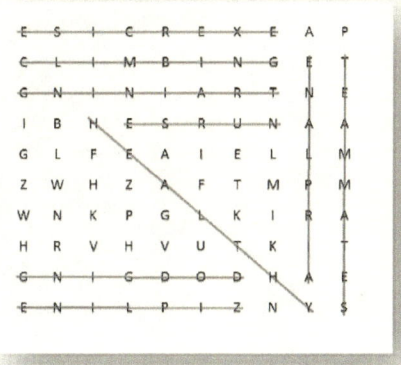

Puzzle 4

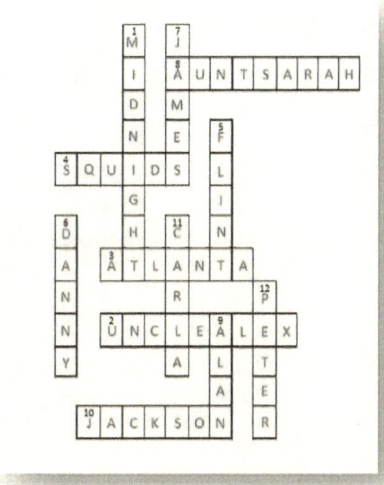

Puzzle 5

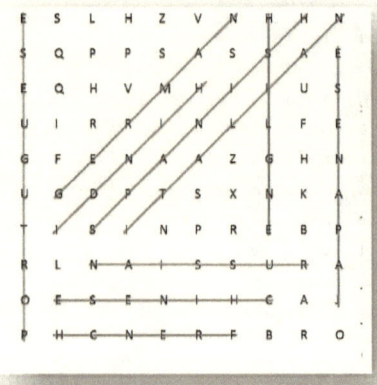

Puzzle 6

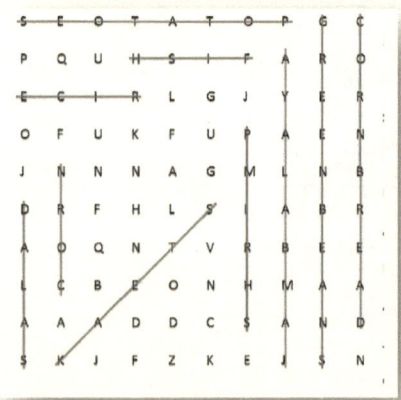

Puzzle 7

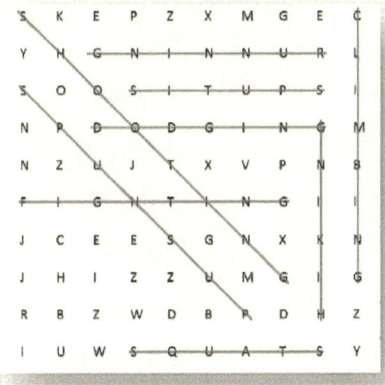

Puzzle 8

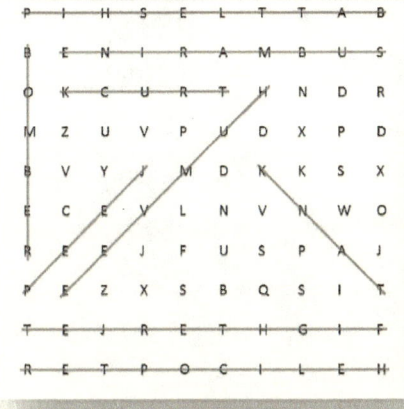

Puzzle 9

1.	WRA	<u>war</u>
2.	IMTRYLIA	<u>military</u>
3.	GTNNIARI	<u>training</u>
4.	MINGCBIL	<u>climbing</u>
5.	IDODGNG	<u>dodging</u>
6.	GFITHGIN	<u>fighting</u>
7.	NUNIRGN	<u>running</u>
8.	NHTOOGSI	<u>shooting</u>
9.	NEUCL XAEL	<u>Uncle Alex</u>
10.	NMTIDHIG	<u>Midnight</u>
11.	RPETE	<u>Peter</u>
12.	LAAN	<u>Alan</u>
13.	SJMAE	<u>James</u>
14.	ATCPNIA IFTLN	<u>Captain Flint</u>
15.	NOAHICSL	<u>Nicholas</u>
16.	COJKANS	<u>Jackson</u>
17.	JEKA	<u>Jake</u>
18.	HNNAAT	<u>Nathan</u>

Puzzle 10

1. UTNA RHSAA — Aunt Sarah
2. ANDNY — Danny
3. TYNO — Tony
4. UKCCH — Chuck
5. 7KA4- — AK-47
6. IHEAMCN GNU — Machine Gun
7. NSHUGOT — Shotgun
8. RTECOK HRNCULAE — Rocket Launcher
9. SUQISD — squids
10. NALATTA — Atlanta
11. IAHOCCG — Chicago
12. TEESRINTTA — Interstate
13. ATKN — tank
14. UKCTR — truck
15. LSPETBHIAT — battleship
16. EBBRMO — bomber
17. HVEOME — homvee
18. PEEJ — jeep

ACKNOWLEDGMENTS

I would like to thank Roya Khosravi, Mrs. Hebert, Mrs. Young, Mrs. Lemoine, and Mr. Koppenol for providing helpful advice during the review process.

COMING SOON IN THE FOUR STRENGTH LIONS SERIES!

Four Strength Lions Book #2- Calling for Help

The soldiers were hunting the whole time until they realized that the bridge was missing. The four lions and the soldiers set out to solve the problem of the missing bridge.

www.ingramcontent.com/pod-product-compliance
Lightning Source LLC
Chambersburg PA
CBHW020617130626
46552CB00003B/1007